CHARISE MERICLE HARPER

GO! GO! GO!
STOP!

ALFRED A. KNOPF 🐕 **NEW YORK**

For Michelle Frey (great editor) and Stephanie Moss (great art director).
Thank you for your patience and *go, go, go* spirit.

THIS IS A BORZOI BOOK PUBLISHED BY ALFRED A. KNOPF

Copyright © 2014 by Charise Mericle Harper

Visit us on the Web! randomhouse.com/kids

Educators and librarians, for a variety of teaching tools,
visit us at RHTeachersLibrarians.com

Library of Congress Cataloging-in-Publication Data
Harper, Charise Mericle.
Go! Go! Go! Stop! / Charise Mericle Harper. — 1st ed.
p.   cm.
Summary: "Little Green only knows one word: 'Go!' It's the perfect thing to get
the construction site moving, but how will they stop?"—Provided by publisher
ISBN 978-0-375-86924-2 (trade)—ISBN 978-0-375-96924-9 (lib. bdg.)—ISBN 978-0-385-75339-5 (ebook)
[1. Traffic signs and signals—Fiction. 2. Construction equipment—Fiction.
3. Bridges—Design and construction—Fiction.] I. Title.
PZ7.H231323Gnm 2014
[E]—dc23
2012046655

MANUFACTURED IN CHINA
March 2014
10 9 8 7 6 5 4 3

First Edition

One day, Little Green said a word.

It was his first word. He had never spoken before.
The word was . . .

He liked how it sounded. He practiced it quiet.

Then medium.

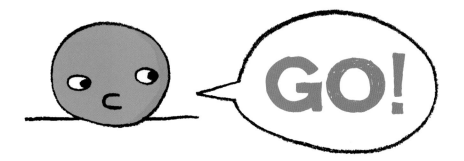

And finally very, very loud.

It was exciting to have a new word.
Little Green couldn't wait to share it.

He bounced into town, jumped to a high place,
and shouted it out for everyone to hear.

It was perfect timing. Naptime was just ending.

Bulldozer was the first to wake up.
"I'm going to surprise Dump Truck," he said,
and he pushed his load of dirt to the top of the hill.

Soon everyone was awake and busy working on the new bridge.

GO! GO! GO! shouted Little Green.

Tow Truck towed terrifically.

Crane carried carefully.

Dump Truck *dumped* dependably.

Mixer mixed marvelously.

And Backhoe waved his long arms in the air.

The more Little Green shouted

the faster everyone moved.

But then . . .

everything got a little crazy.

No one knew what to do.

Little Green tried a whisper,

hoping it would slow things down.

But it only made things worse. And everyone kept going.

Suddenly a stranger rolled into town.

He looked here,   he looked there,

and then he jumped to a high place and
shouted out the only word he knew.

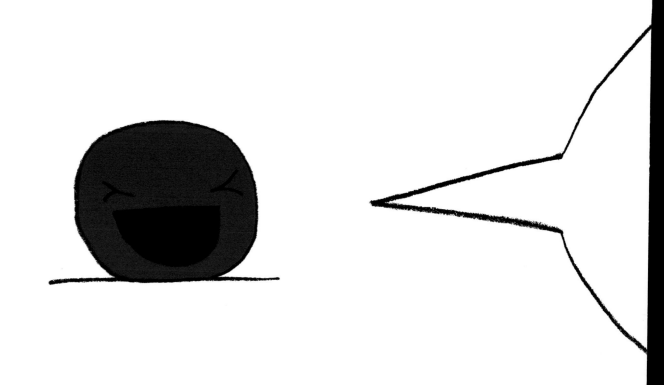

It was just what everyone needed to rest and get organized.

Little Green and Little Red were exact opposites.

But they tried working together.

It wasn't easy.

It wasn't fast.

GO!

STOP, STOP, STOP, STOP, STOP, STOP!

Why are you so far away?

Sorry, too much "Stop!"

But they finally found it.

It was the perfect amount of

to get things done.

Little Green and Little Red liked working together, and they were good at it. The new bridge was finished just on time. Everyone was excited.

"Go!" shouted Little Green, and the cars raced across the bridge.

Then Little Yellow slid into town. He had something to say.

They were the perfect words for a busy bridge.